YOU CHOOSE

SCOOBY-DOO!

THE MYSTERY OF MAYHEM MANSION

STONE ARCH
a capstone imprint

You Choose Stories: Scooby-Doo
is published by Stone Arch Books,
A Capstone Imprint
1710 Roe Crest Drive
North Mankato, Minnesota 56003
www.mycapstone.com

CAPS34844

Cataloging-in-Publication Data is available on the
Library of Congress website.
ISBN: 978-1-4965-2661-8 [Library Hardcover]
ISBN: 978-1-4965-2663-2 [Paperback]
ISBN: 978-1-4965-2665-6 [eBook]

Printed in the United States of America in North Mankato, Minnesota.
092015   00922ICGS16

SCOOBY-DOO!

THE MYSTERY OF
MAYHEM MANSION

written by
Matthew K. Manning

illustrated by
Scott Neely

THE MYSTERY INC. GANG!

SCOOBY-DOO
SKILLS: Loyal; super snout
BIO: This happy-go-lucky hound avoids scary situations at all costs, but he'll do anything for a Scooby Snack!

SHAGGY ROGERS
SKILLS: Lucky; healthy appetite
BIO: This laid-back dude would rather look for grub than search for clues, but he usually finds both!

FRED JONES, JR.
SKILLS: Athletic; charming
BIO: The leader and oldest member of the gang. He's a good sport—and good at them, too!

DAPHNE BLAKE
SKILLS: Brains; beauty
BIO: As a sixteen-year-old fashion queen, Daphne solves her mysteries in style.

VELMA DINKLEY
SKILLS: Clever; highly intelligent
BIO: Although she's the youngest member of Mystery Inc., Velma's an old pro at catching crooks.

SCOOBY-DOO!

Who or what is haunting the ultra-creepy Mayhew Mansion? And who would want to scare away the tourists? Only YOU can help Scooby-Doo and the Mystery Inc. gang solve the mystery.

Follow the directions at the bottom of each page. The choices YOU make will change the outcome of the story. After you finish one path, go back and read the others for more Scooby-Doo adventures!

YOU CHOOSE the path to solve...

THE MYSTERY OF MAYHEM MANSION

The Mystery Machine barely comes to a full stop before Shaggy and Scooby-Doo burst out of the back door of the famous blue van. Shaggy stretches his arms above his head.

"Like, it's good to finally get some fresh air," he says. "I hate being cooped up in that van. It smells like old pizza."

"That's because the only way you and Scooby would come with us on this trip was if we bribed you with six pizzas," says Velma. She slides out the front door of the van and joins her friends.

"Reven," Scooby says.

"It was seven pizzas," says Fred as he and Daphne walk around the other side of the Mystery Machine. "Scooby just ate the first one while we were still packing the van."

Turn the page.

"Since you guys brought it up," says Shaggy, "I wouldn't mind a bite to eat."

Scooby-Doo licks his lips in agreement.

"They might have food inside, guys," says Fred. "But let's get our tickets first."

The Mystery Inc. gang walks up to the large ticket booth. Behind it is a tall wall made completely out of shrubbery. The hedge is well manicured and stands taller than any one of the members of the crime-solving group of teenagers.

Daphne walks up to the ticket counter, but no one seems to be working inside. "Looks closed," she says.

"They have their hours posted on the Internet," Velma says. "The mansion should have opened four minutes ago."

Suddenly, a man pops up from below the window's counter. Daphne jumps backward.

The man in the booth is lanky, with small eyes that remind Daphne of the polished black marbles she used to play with as a young girl.

"Yes?" he says. His voice is a little gruffer than Daphne would like.

"Four tickets to the Mayhew Mansion, please," Daphne says.

"Rive," Scooby-Doo chimes in. He stands on his back legs in order to see into the booth.

"Do dogs need tickets?" Daphne asks.

The man with the beady eyes doesn't answer. He simply types on his register. "That'll be forty dollars," he says.

"I guess that'll remain a mystery," says Velma.

"Yeah, but not nearly as important as the one we're here to solve," says Fred.

Turn the page.

With the tickets in hand, the Mystery Inc. gang walks through the opening in the tall hedge.

"S-s-s-so, do you think this place is really haunted?" asks Shaggy. He shudders just thinking about the idea of running into a ghost.

"That's what the local legends say," says Velma. "They say the Mayhews built the mansion as a maze of sorts to confuse evil spirits."

"Yep," says Fred. "People have reported seeing all types of supernatural things inside the mansion. But we'll get to the bottom of it."

"I'd rather get to the bottom of a chocolate milkshake," Shaggy says as he notices the café outside the mansion's front door.

"Reah! Reah!" Scooby agrees.

But unfortunately for the hungry pair, the rest of the gang doesn't feel the same way. They walk through the mansion's enormous front double doors.

While there were no people outside, the inside of the mansion is surprisingly full of tourists. Scooby and Shaggy catch up with the others as they join a tour group.

"Welcome to the Mayhew Mansion," says the tour guide. She's a short woman with curly hair. She has an expression on her face that looks like she's been at this job far too long. "Let's begin, shall we?" she says in a bland, bored tone.

The tour guide leads the procession up the impressive twisting stairs from the lobby to the first floor. The Mystery Inc. gang takes up the rear.

"As you can see, the Mayhew Mansion is known for its eccentric architecture," says the tour guide, in a bored, half-asleep tone. "And the family behind the house's creation is just as exciting," she says.

"I'm not sure if she knows what the word *exciting* means," says Velma to Daphne.

Daphne laughs.

Turn the page.

"Famous comedians Jeffrey Mayhew and Madeline Mayhew built the mansion in 1888," drones the tour guide. "Now owned by the state of California, the house's last known occupants were failed horror filmmaker Tina Mayhew and her brother Timothy."

The Mystery Inc. gang follows the guide down a dark hallway.

"It's said that Timothy ran away with a traveling circus before his untimely death," says the tour guide. "Likewise, Tina disappeared in disgrace. No one has seen them since. Their ghosts have been rumored to walk these halls to this day."

"If we're going to get to the bottom of this mystery," whispers Fred, "we better explore the house ourselves."

"I think we should stay with the group," says Velma.

"Like, I'm still not sure why we didn't stop at the café," says Shaggy nervously.

To follow Fred and Daphne upstairs, go to page 13.
To follow Velma and the tour, turn to page 14.
To follow Scooby and Shaggy to the café, turn to page 16.

When the tour guide turns around to lead the large group, Daphne and Fred run to the nearby staircase. There's a red rope blocking it off. They jump it quickly, sprint upstairs, and find themselves in another hallway.

"Look at this place!" Fred says.

To their left, the hall is bright and well lit. The tile is perfectly clean and shiny. There are several doors lining the hallway, each with beautiful marble doorknobs.

To their right, the hallway is dark and eerie. A few broken chairs lean against the wall. It looks like they haven't been dusted in years. A thick, shag carpet covers the floor that might be the home to any number of small insects. An ominous, dark wooden door stands at the far end of the hallway.

"It's like the house has a split personality," says Daphne.

If Fred and Daphne go **left**, turn to page **18**.
If Fred and Daphne go **right**, turn to page **25**.

Velma works her way to the front of the tour, as her friends head off in different directions.

"Now if you'll follow me, we'll see something really thrilling," says the tour guide in her flat tone.

The group shuffles into a small, confined room. There are no windows. Only an antique candelabrum lights the chamber, complete with real, slowly melting candles.

"This is the séance room," says the guide. "The Mayhew Mansion was created to confuse evil spirits. This room played a large part in that."

"I didn't know the Mayhews were so superstitious," says Velma.

"Not superstitious," the guide says, her tone changing for the first time since the tour began. Now she sounds frightened, almost for her very life. "They were completely right," she whispers to Velma.

The tour guide instantly regains her monotone voice. "If anyone would like to experience the séance chamber like the Mayhews, please remain in the room," she says. "The candles will be snuffed in order to draw the supernatural elements close. The rest of the guests are invited to follow me to the drawing room."

Velma looks up at the candles.

She watches as the small flames jump and dance. Shadows flicker across the ceiling like living things. She feels the tiny hairs rise on the back of her neck.

"Gulp," Velma says, despite herself.

If Velma stays in the séance room, turn to page 21.

If Velma heads to the drawing room, turn to page 27.

Shaggy and Scooby-Doo head for the café. They stop and stare at a sign in front of them.

"Now this is my type of mystery," says Shaggy.

"Re, roo!" says Scooby, nodding his head.

The sign reads: "Ice Cream Flavors of the Day: Chocolate, Vanilla, and Mystery Flavor!"

"But why stop at just ice cream, old buddy?" says Shaggy as he saunters over to a small round table at the outdoor café. "I think we have time for a standard twelve-course meal."

No sooner does Shaggy sit down, than a waiter approaches him. The waiter is a lean, middle-aged man with slick, black hair, dressed in a tuxedo.

"I'm sorry, sir," says the waiter. "No animals in the café."

"Like, what?" says Shaggy. "Scooby's not an animal! He's like family."

"Reah!" Scooby chimes in. "Ramily!"

"Sorry, sir," says the waiter. "You and your . . . family . . . will have to go somewhere else."

"I'm not gonna take this sitting down!" says Shaggy.

"Or randing up!" adds Scooby. The two storm off toward the mansion's front entrance.

Once inside, Shaggy approaches the information desk. "Like, I wanna make a complaint about a really snooty waiter!" says Shaggy.

"Of course, sir," says an elderly man at the front desk. "Which one?"

"He was a skinny guy with black hair," says Shaggy.

"In a ruxredo!" adds Scooby.

The old man mulls over the information for a moment and then says, "I'm sorry, sir. We don't have anyone like that on staff. We had someone that met that description when the café first opened, but that was over sixty years ago. I remember he gave me a tour on my first day at work."

If Shaggy and Scooby investigate the mystery waiter, turn to page 23.

If Shaggy and Scooby go back to the café to eat, turn to page 29.

Fred and Daphne step onto the slick tile floor of the hallway. To either side, pewter art deco lamps light their way, making the freshly painted white walls look all the brighter.

"So the question is, which way next?" says Fred. Daphne looks around them. There are several doors down the hall, and one right next to her. She tries the knob, but it's locked.

A gust of cold wind drifts down the hall. Daphne shivers.

"Turn around," says a voice from down the hall.

Daphne and Fred both look, but they can't see anyone.

"Where did that voice—" Daphne starts to say, but is interrupted when another cold wind whips by her. The wind is stronger this time.

"Someone doesn't want us poking around," says Fred.

"Maybe we should listen," says Daphne.

"That doesn't sound like us," says Fred.

Fred smiles at Daphne, and all she can manage is a half-grin in return. The two continue down the bright hallway. They walk a little slower than before. Fred tries the door on the right. . . .

He and Daphne continue down the bright hallway. Fred tries the door on the right, while Daphne twists the knob of the door on the left. *CLICK!* Both doors open easily.

"This way," says Fred.

"I think the voice was coming from my door," says Daphne.

The two look at each other. They know they have to split up.

To follow Fred, turn to page 32.
To follow Daphne, turn to page 48.

Velma does her best to remain calm as the tour guide walks past her, holding the long, brass candlesnuffer. One by one, the guide puts the candles out. The room grows darker and darker. Soon, Velma can see only the silhouette of the tour guide in the doorway, lit from the drawing room behind her.

"Your time alone in the séance room will begin now," she says in her flat voice. "For the sake of the other guests, please keep your screaming to a minimum."

"My screaming?" Velma says, but the guide has left the room already, shutting the door behind her.

Velma looks around the chamber. It is so dark that she can't even see her hand in front of her face.

Turn the page.

Velma wonders when her eyes will start to adjust. But she doesn't have much time to ponder that particular question. Because seconds later, she notices a faint white light coming from behind her in the corner of the room.

Velma spins around and sees a white figure standing in front of her. It is tall, with long, glowing white limbs and a monstrous expression on its face.

She steps back and bumps into the wall. Her glasses fall to the floor.

If Velma searches for her glasses, turn to page 34.

If Velma runs out of the room without her glasses, turn to page 52.

"Like, I know what I saw," says Shaggy as he and Scooby head back to the café. "Let's find out exactly who that waiter was."

"Reah!" says Scooby, feeling particularly brave.

Shaggy and Scooby stop at the entrance to the café and look around. It's a fairly small eatery, located right off the main entrance to the mansion. The seating is all outdoors, with various black metal tables sprinkled here and there on the cobblestone patio. The kitchen is actually a part of the manor itself. The waiters and waitresses enter and exit through a busy side door, carrying cold, empty plates or full, piping-hot ones.

Just then, Scooby sees their mystery waiter heading toward the corner of the mansion, past the kitchen door.

"Raggy, rook!" he shouts.

Turn the page.

"Like, look at what?" asks Shaggy.

"Raiter!" says Scooby, pointing with one paw. "Rover there!"

It takes Shaggy a few seconds, but he finally looks where Scooby is pointing, just in time to see the waiter disappear around the corner.

"Should we follow him?" asks Shaggy.

Scooby shrugs. Things never seem to go well when he and Shaggy try to solve a mystery on their own.

"Maybe we should get the gang," says Shaggy.

Scooby shrugs again.

The waiter is now completely out of sight. They need to act fast.

If Scooby and Shaggy follow the waiter, turn to page 36.

If Scooby and Shaggy try to find the rest of the gang, turn to page 55.

It doesn't take long for Fred and Daphne to cross the entire length of the dimly lit hallway.

"So I guess we go in here," says Daphne as she turns the handle of the door at the hall's far end.

"Guess so," Fred says. He tries to sound confident, but he can't help feeling a little nervous. There is something odd about this part of the mansion. Something he can't describe. There is a feeling in the air that makes Fred feel like he shouldn't be there.

CREEEEEAAAAAKKKK.

In front of them is a staircase that winds up and turns a corner. The two each take a deep breath and then begin to climb the stairs.

Turn the page.

"What is this place?" Daphne says as they step into a room at the top of the stairs.

Fred doesn't answer. Despite all the cases the Mystery Inc. gang has investigated, he has never seen anything like this. It's all he can do to not let out a quiet gasp. The room he is standing in is absolutely mammoth. But that's not the strange part. Not by a long shot. The strange part is the stairs.

The stairs are everywhere. Staircases head up to the story above, and some lead to the floor below. And oddly, there are stairs built into the walls, going sideways. Even the ceiling has a staircase hanging from it. Fred walks up to one of the sets of sideways stairs and examines them.

"Up or down?" Daphne asks.

If Fred and Daphne take a stairway up, turn to page **68.**
If Fred and Daphne take a stairway down, turn to page **86.**

Velma shivers as she follows the others into the drawing room. She's not about to voluntarily lock herself in a dark, unfamiliar room. She may be curious about the ghost stories of this old house, but she's not *that* curious.

"So we're all here then," says the tour guide with her usual lack of enthusiasm. "Wonderful. Let's continue, shall we?"

The group shuffles up a few flights of stairs and onto a large rooftop patio. All the while, the tour guide drones on. "The stories of the hauntings of the Mayhew Mansion are many. Some have reported seeing strange, white glowing figures, or even ghostly creatures that take the form of gigantic animals. Despite the Mayhews' attempts at making the mansion a virtual maze of clashing designs and winding hallways, hundreds of these stories still abound."

Turn the page.

The tour guide stands in front of the ledge of the patio. Behind her, Velma can see the elaborate gardens that comprise the building's side yard.

"In fact, some guests report there being possess—" the guide begins to say, but a sudden coughing fit stops her in mid-sentence. "Possess—" she tries to say again. "Possess*IONS!*" she finally says. But the end of the word seems very different than the beginning. Gone is the guide's boring monotone. Now she's talking in a monstrous, deep voice. *"Possessions like this one!"* she yells. Her eyes begin to glow with bright white light. Velma looks around as the other tourists start to scatter to different corners of the roof. Everyone is terrified!

If Velma tries to help the guide, turn to page 71.

If Velma runs, turn to page 89.

"Like, that sure was weird, huh, Scoob?" says Shaggy as they both head back to the café. "But even a creepy old ghost can't scare away my appetite."

The two sit down at a table near the mansion's outer wall. Behind them is a row of dark windows lining a closed section of the giant building.

A waitress brings over a menu, but Shaggy waves it away. "We already know what we want," he says. "Bring us a dozen hot dogs and four chocolate shakes, please."

"Rix!" Scooby says.

"Six chocolate shakes," says Shaggy.

"Uh . . . okay," says the waitress, raising an eyebrow before turning away.

Turn the page.

"What were we even worried about?" says Shaggy. "Just 'cause some snooty guy can't take our order?"

"Rilly," says Scooby.

"It is silly," says Shaggy. "Just because he happens to look like someone who used to work here sixty years ago, doesn't mean the place is crawling with ghosts!"

But Scooby doesn't answer. He just stares behind him at the mansion's nearby windows.

"Right, Scoob?" asks Shaggy.

Scooby's eyes are wide now. He looks terrified.

"Scooby?" Shaggy asks again as he turns around to see what his pal is looking at. In the window behind them stands a little boy. He is wearing clothing that looks as if it belongs in the 1800s. His face is emotionless. Scooby and Shaggy blink, and the boy is gone.

If Scooby and Shaggy decide to do nothing, turn to page 73.
If Scooby and Shaggy run, turn to page 92.

Fred turns away from Daphne and walks through the door in front of him.

"Whoa," he says.

He knows better, but Fred could swear he is standing in an actual cave. There are stalactites above him and stalagmites lining the uneven gray floor. He feels the wall. It's cold to the touch, like stone. It even feels a little moist, like the real caverns he's been in on occasion.

"Pretty neat, huh?" says a voice from behind him.

Fred turns to see a small elderly man, leaning on a cane.

"Don't worry," says the old man. "I won't tell anyone you're up here. Although you shouldn't be."

"Oh," says Fred. "Um . . . thanks."

"I'm doing the same thing, truth be told," says the man.

"Really?" says Fred. Something about this old man is off-putting, but Fred can't put his finger on it. He seems friendly enough.

"Sure," says the old man. "I've been coming here for years. Sneaking around these strange rooms. I have a personal interest in this sort of thing. I'm an architect, you see."

"So did you help build this place?" asks Fred.

"Oh, no. That was before my time, son," says the elderly man. "But it's a fascinating building. Apparently, the Mayhews were a superstitious lot. Built all these twists and turns to ward off evil spirits. To keep 'em confused."

Turn to page 38.

Velma quickly drops to her knees and begins feeling for her glasses. Out of the corner of her eye, she can see the fuzzy image of the glowing, lanky figure coming toward her. But she can't waste time on that. If she doesn't find her glasses, she won't be able to solve this mystery.

Finally, she finds the glasses and puts them on. But the ghost is nowhere to be seen. It has somehow disappeared.

"Jinkies," says Velma. "That's strange."

Velma feels another shiver run through her. She knows better than to believe in things like ghosts—it's hard not to trust her own eyes. But the moment passes as quickly as it came.

From being in the dark so long, Velma's eyes have started to adjust. She notices a faint glowing, white light coming from a crack in a nearby wall.

Velma runs her fingers over the smooth outline of the wall of the séance room. The wall is cold and slick. It feels as unwelcoming as the tour guide acts. Eventually, she feels a crack so large her fingertips can slide inside it. She puts both hands in the opening and pulls. There is a loud clicking noise, followed by the creak of an ancient hinge. The wall swings open, revealing a winding staircase. At the bottom of the staircase, Velma can see a hint of the white light that had surrounded the lanky "ghost."

"Oh, boy," Velma says under her breath. She lets out a sigh. "Nothing ventured, nothing gained, I guess."

Then she starts down the stairs. . .

Turn to page 42.

Shaggy and Scooby look at each other for a moment. Letting out a collective, nervous sigh, they then hustle after the mysterious waiter. But when they turn the corner around the side of the mansion, the sight before them isn't exactly inviting.

Without knowing it, Scooby and Shaggy have entered the Mayhew Mansion's gardens. As detailed and elaborate as the rest of the famous mansion, the gardens are comprised mostly of a giant hedge maze.

The maze has two main entrances and towers above even Shaggy's head. It appears nearly as intimidating as the mansion itself.

Scooby looks up at the tall hedge. "Gulp!" he says.

"Like, that goes double for me, ol' pal," says Shaggy. "Here's hoping your ol' sniffer is up to snuff."

Scooby-Doo begins to sniff the ground.

"Ris ray!" he shouts and then takes off into the maze. Not wanting to be left alone in the rather creepy, shadowy gardens, Shaggy follows.

"Like, wait up, Scoobs!" Shaggy calls.

The hedge maze is full of twists and turns. But none of them slows Scooby down. He's locked onto a scent, and he fully intends to follow it, even if Shaggy isn't quite happy with their current pace.

After turning a final corner, Scooby slows down. Shaggy nearly punches a teen-sized hole through the hedge but manages to stop himself as suddenly as his canine buddy.

"What did ya' find, pal?" huffs Shaggy, as he steps out into a clearing.

Turn to page 45.

Fred looks around at the walls of the man-made cavern. "This place certainly is confusing," he says.

"As well it should be," says the man. "That's why I'm glad you came along."

"Me?" says Fred.

"Sure," says the elderly man. "We spirits can't get around as well as you living folks."

"Spirits?" says Fred.

As the man speaks, Fred notices that his eyes are starting to glow white. In fact, the man's entire body seems to be glowing now.

"What . . . what are you?" asks Fred.

"I'm trapped, is what I am," says the man. His feet slowly lift off the floor. Fred's eyes go wide. Whatever this ghost wants, Fred wants no part of it.

Fred turns and runs across the length of the makeshift cave. He runs under an arched doorway and into the next room. It seems to be some sort of workshop. There are stained-glass panels leaning against the walls. But Fred doesn't have time to admire the artistry. Instead, he crosses the room in a hurry, heading toward a closed door.

Fred's hand reaches for the knob. It's locked. Suddenly, he hears a voice whisper in his ear. "What's the rush, son?" says the elderly man.

"Yikes!" says Fred.

Turning, Fred doesn't see the old man anywhere. Then he spots him. The white figure is floating toward him from the arched doorway. Fred sees another door to his left and rushes toward it.

Turn the page.

"You shouldn't be in here," barks a voice in front of Fred.

Blocking his path is a rather large security guard. He doesn't look happy.

"I . . . " Fred says as he checks behind him for any trace of the elderly ghost. But there's nothing there. "I . . . but . . . ," is all Fred can muster.

"But nothing, kid," says the guard. "I already caught your friends snooping around. Consider yourselves banned from the Mayhew Mansion."

The guard takes Fred by the arm and leads him down a nearby staircase. All the while, Fred keeps looking over his shoulder. But there is no sign of the ghost. Fred thinks that maybe he should tell the guard about what he's seen. But as Fred joins the rest of the Mystery Inc. gang outside the mansion's large hedge, he's just glad to get out of that house for good. And from the looks on his friends' faces, he isn't the only one.

THE END

To follow another path, turn to page 12.

At the bottom of the stairs, Velma turns the corner into an old cellar of some sort. The walls are made of stone and feel cold. The floor beneath her is made of large gray cobblestones. There are old wooden shelves mounted to the walls, each holding cans of paint. And the reason Velma can see all of this is because the paint cans are open, and their contents are glowing brightly.

"Glow-in-the-dark paint," says Velma. "Interesting."

Across the cellar from her is a wooden door. Velma walks over to it and pushes it open slowly.

On the other side of the door is a tunnel that looks almost like a mineshaft.

Velma rifles through a nearby shelf before discovering a small glass jar. She takes the jar and pours some of the glow-in-the-dark paint into it. Then she heads back over to the mineshaft and slowly steps inside.

Five minutes later, Velma reaches the mineshaft's other end. There's a closed wooden door above her and a ladder leading up to it. Luckily the door is not locked. Velma pushes it open with a quick shove. Suddenly the brilliant afternoon sun is shining down on her.

She crawls up into a large, well-kept field. Around her are several more buckets of the glow-in-the-dark paint. They're all opened.

"Looks like someone's charging another batch of paint," she says.

Velma looks across the pasture and sees a familiar sight. It's the large hedge that surrounds the mansion grounds. She walks closer to it and sees a small opening.

Pushing through the bushes, Velma finds herself behind the ticket booth. There are bushes everywhere. It's a very secluded place, which explains why the lanky ticket taker is currently using it to change out of his ghost costume.

"Ahem," says Velma.

Turn the page.

The ticket manager turns to see her with his beady eyes. "Oh," he says. "Um . . . I'll be right with you?"

Later, when Velma shows the rest of the Mystery Inc. gang the "ghost's" changing area, she smiles as she explains. "So the ticket manager faked it all," she says. "Apparently, the mansion made more money when people thought it was haunted."

"Like that's—" Shaggy starts to say.

CLLAAANNNGG!!!

At the loud sound, Shaggy leaps up into Velma's arms in pure fear. Behind him, Scooby-Doo is lying on the ground, now covered in the glowing white paint, with an overturned paint can on his head.

"Scooby!" Velma says. She tries to sound stern but can't help smiling.

"Rorry!" Scooby says. But Velma can't hear him over the sound of her friends' laughter.

THE END

To follow another path, turn to page 12.

Scooby-Doo and Shaggy walk into the large clearing, right at the center of the hedge maze. There are a few benches around an impressive oak tree. But there is little else at the maze's center besides a fountain that looks to have stopped working decades ago.

"Rhere!" says Scooby. He narrows his eyes and points his body at one of the benches. There's a lone figure sitting on the small wooden bench. He is facing the hedges with his back to Scooby and Shaggy. He is still and quiet. Nervous, Shaggy slowly approaches the bench. Scooby follows, making sure he stays behind his friend. Shaggy does his best not to shake like a leaf as he extends his hand to touch the man's shoulder.

Scooby's eyes go wide.

Turn the page.

Shaggy taps the shoulder of the man on the bench. The man turns his head to look at Shaggy and Scooby.

"Can I help you?" asks the man.

Shaggy has never seen him before. The man stands up. He is a large, muscular gentleman with a shaved head. He is wearing a tight-fitting shirt with a badge pinned on it that reads "Security."

"Like, Scoobs, this isn't the right guy," says Shaggy. Scooby narrows his eyes again and points at the man's hand.

Shaggy looks at what the man is holding.

In the security guard's hand is a half-eaten hot dog.

"Scooby!" says Shaggy. "You were supposed to be following the scent of that creepy waiter, not following your stomach!"

Scooby looks at Shaggy and then lunges forward and chomps the remainder of the hot dog right out of the guard's hand.

"Now you've done it!" says Shaggy as he turns to run. But before he and Scooby can even move a few inches, the guard grabs both of their collars.

"That's it!" he says as he drags them back through the maze toward the entrance. "Consider yourselves banned from the Mayhew Mansion!"

Later Scooby-Doo and Shaggy have no choice but to wait for their friends in the Mystery Machine.

"Well you botched the case, Scoobs," says Shaggy. "I hope that hot dog was worth it."

Scooby doesn't answer. He just licks his lips and smiles.

THE END

To follow another path, turn to page 12.

Daphne shakes her head as she looks around the room. She had been sure that the voice she and Fred had heard came from this direction. But there is absolutely nothing in the room. No furniture, no windows. There's not even a door besides the one Daphne has walked in through. And even that door doesn't have a doorframe.

SLAM!

Daphne spins around. The door behind her has slammed shut. The back of the door has been painted white. It is so smooth that it blends in with the rest of the wall almost perfectly. In fact, it was difficult to even see the tiny crack around the doorframe.

"I hope that was the wind," Daphne says.

As she stares at the door, she realizes that it has no knob.

"How am I supposed to get out of here?" she says.

Daphne's eyes dart around the empty room again. Perhaps this part of the mansion is off-limits for good reason. She walks over to the wall on the opposite side of the room. It's just a blank white wall. She looks up at the ceiling. It's flat and white, too. Even the lights are just flat panels in the ceiling.

She lets out a sigh and leans on the wall behind her. And all of a sudden, she loses her balance. By just putting a little weight on it, the entire wall has slid backward, just a foot, revealing a section of the floor painted jet black.

"That's strange," mutters Daphne.

Daphne bends down and touches the black floor. Then she stands up, looks at the sliding wall, and pushes it harder.

Turn the page.

The wall slides back a few feet before Daphne can't push it anymore.

CLICK!

There on the black floor beside Daphne, a trapdoor springs open. By pushing the wall as far back as it could go, she's unlocked some sort of secret chamber. It's dark inside the perfectly square hole, but Daphne doesn't have much choice. She can see the top of a ladder, so she gingerly places one foot on it and then the next. She's careful not to lose her balance as she moves. The rungs are so thin, it feels like they could snap beneath her at any moment.

But Daphne continues down, making sure her grip is tight on each new rung. She climbs down into the darkness.

"I hope Fred's having better luck than I am," she says to herself.

Turn to page 58.

Although everything looks fuzzy without her glasses, Velma manages to find the door to the séance room. She throws it open and runs into the drawing room. But as far as she can tell, the tour has moved on. It's hard to be sure, though. Everything just looks like blobs of color without her glasses.

She looks over her shoulder and sees a familiar white blob.

"Jinkies!" she shouts. "The ghost!"

Velma opens the closest door and runs inside. She slams it shut behind her and looks around. There are colorful blobs everywhere. She stays still for a moment just to make sure that none of them is moving. Once she's sure she's alone, she walks over to touch one of the blobs. She instantly recognizes the object. It's a book.

"I'm in the library," she says.

Feeling her way across the room with the bookcase as her guide, Velma moves as fast as she can. But when her hand touches a large brown book, the book slides forward. Suddenly the wall swivels around, and Velma finds herself swiveling right along with it. She does her best to hold on. The wall and floor are spinning at an incredibly fast rate.

Velma's now standing in a completely different room. It's much brighter than the dimly lit library but she still can't see anything other than fuzzy shapes without her glasses. She walks forward and bumps into a table.

"Hey!" says a voice from her left.

Velma turns to see a white blob.

"The ghost!" she shouts.

Turn the page.

Velma can't remember a time when she ran this quickly. She shoots from one side of the room to the opposite in less time than it takes her to think about it. Unfortunately, her quick sprint is soon interrupted when she trips over a bed. Her momentum causes her to roll off the bed onto the floor.

Velma peers under the bed and sees what must be the ghost's legs as it floats closer to her. To Velma's unfocused eyes, the legs look like two skinny blue lines.

Fearing for her life, Velma quickly gets to her feet again. She spies the bedroom's doorway, runs toward it, and feels her way down a large staircase.

Turn to page 62.

"Like, let's go find the others," says Shaggy. He and Scooby head inside the Mayhew Mansion.

"*Brrrrr*," says Scooby as they walk through the large double front doors. The inside of the lobby is enough to run a chill down anyone's spine. Scooby hadn't taken the time to notice how creepy the inside of the mansion really is. The floor is made up of a cold marble. A giant, claw-like chandelier hangs above them. Windows in sharp, ominous shapes line the outer wall.

"So the question is, like, where did they skedaddle to?" says Shaggy. Shaggy looks over at one of the large archways to his left. It is labeled "West Wing."

"Guess we'll just wing it!" Shaggy says.

Scooby follows his friend, but can't help but shake his head at his awful joke.

Turn the page.

In the West Wing, Scooby's ears perk up. While the room is empty, he can hear a conversation nearby.

"You hear that, too?" Shaggy asks his friend.

Scooby nods. The two move slowly toward the voices. There are no other doors in the room, but there is a row of sharp-arched windows. Shaggy stands on his tiptoes. He can just see out through a small crack in the stained glass. Scooby props himself up on his hind legs to see out, too.

It takes Scooby a few minutes to gain his balance. After almost falling over on top of his human friend, Scooby-Doo finally peers out through the crack.

"Ruh-roh!" Scooby says.

"Gulp! It's the waiter!" Shaggy says. Through the small crack, Shaggy can just see the mystery waiter talking to a few other men in tuxedos, as well as a few women dressed as maids.

"Ris he a rhost?" Scooby asks.

"Like, how should I know if he's a ghost," says Shaggy. "He looks pretty alive to me."

The waiter begins to talk to his friends. Shaggy can just make out what he's saying. "Think I got rid of another couple tourists," he says. "Some skinny hippie and his dog."

"Hippie?" says Shaggy. "I thought these pants were slimming."

"*Shhhh!*" Scooby says, still listening.

"I managed to get some grade school teacher and his class pretty mad," says one of the women dressed like a maid. "Refused to tell 'em where the bathroom was."

"We're getting there," says another man in a tuxedo.

As Scooby and Shaggy continue to spy on the well-dressed staff outside, neither sees a hand reaching out for Shaggy's shoulder.

Turn to page 65.

The light from the room above Daphne shuts off as soon as she is halfway down the ladder, as if triggered by her weight.

"What?!?" Daphne says without actually meaning to. She freezes for a moment. Should she keep going or head back up into the white room? Daphne sighs. It's not like she has much of a choice. She needs to find an exit.

Daphne steels herself and continues down the ladder. She knows she has reached the bottom when her feet touch the floor beneath her. That's the only indication, though. The room is so dark that Daphne can only navigate by touch.

But she isn't about to stop now. She puts her hands out in front of her. She doesn't feel anything, so she keeps walking. Then her fingertips feel something familiar. It's a light switch.

CLICK.

Daphne's shoulders droop when she sees the room around her.

The room is completely black. Only white light from the ceiling panel interrupts the otherwise jet black room. There's no furniture, windows, or doors. Again.

"Really?" Daphne says. She's more than a little annoyed. But she wastes no time, this time around. She walks across the room and shoves the wall. It doesn't budge. So she heads to the next wall and pushes it. Nothing. She has the same luck with the third wall. It's not until she shoves on the last one that anything happens.

Just like the room above, the wall slides forward. And once again, there's a click. But the click isn't a trapdoor opening in the white floor exposed by the moving wall. The click is coming from the wall itself this time. A doorknob pops forward from seemingly out of nowhere.

Daphne twists the knob and pushes the door forward.

She steps through the doorway without thinking about it.

Turn the page.

It's too late when Daphne realizes that she's falling. The door leads to the outside, and a two-story drop to the backyard below. Daphne screams, but she barely has time. Her body is already splashing into a huge swimming pool.

When she climbs out of the water, she sees the large man standing in front of her. The badge on his chest tells her that this man is a security guard. The frown on his face tells her she's about to leave the Mayhew Mansion in a hurry.

Daphne straightens her skirt as she walks toward the Mystery Machine in the parking lot to wait for her friends. She's always liked the van's bright color scheme, but today, she's just happy to see anything that's not so black and white.

THE END

To follow another path, turn to page 12.

After a few more stumbles and one rather dangerous fall, Velma reaches the bottom of the staircase. She hears a commotion to her left and sees a group of fuzzy, multicolored blobs approaching her.

It must be a tour group, Velma thinks.

She turns around and peers back up the stairs. The ghost is still fast approaching.

"Run!" Velma yells to the tour group. "There's a ghost!"

But the group doesn't move. And the ghost keeps getting closer.

"What's the matter with you people?!" shouts Velma. There's no time to stay and argue. The ghost is halfway down the steps.

"Stop!" the ghost yells from behind Velma. It sounds eerily familiar, but Velma is not about to do what it says. She runs past the tour group and out the front door. Velma is so scared that she doesn't even look back until she's past the large hedges out in front of the mansion.

It's only then that she peers over her shoulder. Not looking where she's going, she runs right into someone standing in front of her.

"Like, Velma?" says a fuzzy figure that couldn't be anyone other than Shaggy. "Where are your glasses?"

"There's no time for that now!" shouts Velma. "Look!"

She points to the white blob of a figure hovering toward them. It is still following her and is almost through the gates.

"The ghost!" says Velma.

"G-g-ghost?" says Shaggy. "Gulp! Where?"

"Rhost?" says Scooby, who is now standing by Shaggy's side.

"He's right there!" shouts Velma. And indeed, the white, blurry figure is just a few steps away. Then the ghost speaks.

Turn the page.

"Velma, what's wrong? I've been trying to catch up with you since I saw you in the drawing room," says Fred. "Here, I found your glasses."

The white blurry figure holds out his hand to Velma. She takes the glasses and puts them on. Sure enough, the white blur had been Fred the entire time

"So, uh . . ." says Fred. "You okay?"

"Well, don't I feel ridiculous," Velma says.

"Let's head back in and find out what's really going on in the mansion," Fred says. But Shaggy and Scooby are already in the Mystery Machine.

"For once, I'm with Scooby and Shaggy," says Velma. With that, she climbs in the back of the van, and Fred can only wonder what Velma saw in that séance room.

THE END

To follow another path, turn to page 12.

"Zoinks!" Shaggy yells as the mysterious hand touches his shoulder.

Shaggy and Scooby-Doo both spin around from the window to see Fred, Velma, and Daphne standing behind them.

"Whoa, Shaggy!" says Fred. "It's only us."

"I hope you guys had better luck getting to the bottom of this mystery than we have," says Velma.

"Like, you're in luck," says Shaggy. "See those guys outside? I don't think any of them work here. But they act like they do."

Fred stands on his tiptoes and looks out the crack. "Where?" he says. "There's no one there."

Shaggy peers out the window again. "Like, unless Scoob and I are seriously cracking up, those guys just split!"

Turn the page.

"Let's get outside!" says Fred.

The Mystery Inc. gang runs out of the West Wing and through the lobby. They sprint out the front door and past the café. Then they turn the corner into the mansion's side yard. There's a large hedge maze to their left. Just as Shaggy and Scooby are about to run inside it, Fred points to a small gardener's shed in the other direction. The mystery waiter is walking into the shed. He shuts the door behind him without seeing the gang.

"That's him!" shouts Shaggy.

"Reah! Rat's rim!" Scooby agrees.

The gang runs over to the shed. Daphne tries the door. It's unlocked. She slowly pushes the wooden door open on its rusty hinges.

In the shed are the waiters and maids. They're getting ready to leave the mansion grounds.

"Um," says the mystery waiter. "We're closed."

"Do any of you even work here?" asks Fred.

"I can answer that," says a shaky voice from behind them. It's the elderly man who works at the mansion's information desk. "And the answer is no."

"Then, like, who are they?" asks Shaggy.

"They work for the Walcram Hotel chain," says the old man. "They're trying to chase away our visitors so the mansion makes less money and goes out of business. They've had their eye on the Mayhew Mansion for generations."

"And we would've gotten away with it, if it weren't for—" the skinny waiter starts to say.

"We've heard that one before," says Velma. "Now if you'll excuse us, there's a café in need of our tourist dollars."

As the gang walks away, Shaggy adds, "And a few stomachs in need of some milkshakes."

THE END

To follow another path, turn to page 12.

"Let's go up, Daphne," says Fred.

Fred leads the way as he and Daphne begin to walk up one of the sets of stairs in the massive ballroom. Suddenly, Fred feels Daphne clutch his arm.

"Look!" she shouts.

"What?" Fred says.

Daphne's grip tightens around Fred's arm. He looks up. Skittering down a set of stairs on the ceiling is a giant spider. It's about twice Fred's size and easily five times as angry. The hairy black thing turns its head a bit to the side. It's like it's sizing up its soon-to-be dinner. Fred freezes in his tracks. He's never seen anything like this monster. It's an amazing thing to see.

A few seconds later, he comes to his senses. "Run!" Fred yells. But Daphne is way ahead of him.

Deciding Daphne has the right idea, Fred runs after her. They dart off the stairs into a tight hallway with a low ceiling. At the end of the hall are two open doorways. Without really debating the issue, Daphne turns to the right, and Fred follows her.

It's not until they're completely through the doorway that the two realize how strange their surroundings are yet again. The room around them is completely painted to look like the outdoors. Although they know they're still inside the mansion, the walls are so intricately detailed, Fred and Daphne could swear they are standing in a thick forest.

Fred pops his head back out the doorway and then ducks back in the room. "I don't see that spider, or whatever it was," he says. "I think we lost it."

Turn to page 75.

Velma cautiously approaches the tour guide.

"Are you okay?" she asks.

The tour guide cocks her head to the side. She looks a bit like a lion, sizing up its next meal. Her eyes stare at Velma with an intense gaze. She doesn't blink. It looks to Velma like she's forgotten how.

"ARRH!!!" the guide yells. White light pours from inside her open mouth. The same white light shoots out of her eyes.

"So, that's a no then," Velma says. She begins to back away from the guide. But before she's more than a yard away from the woman, the guide charges directly at her.

Turn the page.

Velma's heart pounds. Every impulse is telling her to run, but she stands her ground. The tour guide isn't stopping, though.

"Wait!" Velma yells. "This isn't you! Something is controlling your body!"

But the guide isn't listening either.

Out of pure instinct, Velma ducks down just as the guide reaches her.

CLANK!

The tour guide topples over Velma and lands face first on the floor of the patio.

"Oof," the guide says.

"Are you okay?" Velma asks.

The tour guide doesn't move.

Velma slowly rolls the woman over, afraid of what she's about to see.

Turn to page 79.

"Ruh-ruh!" Scooby-Doo says, shaking his head no.

"Yeah, I don't think we should chase after him, either," says Shaggy. "Odds are that little boy was another creepy ghost."

"What little boy?" asks Fred as he walks up behind Scooby and Shaggy from inside the mansion's front door. Daphne and Velma are close behind him.

"Oh, great," says Shaggy. "Now they're totally gonna make us."

"Make you do what?" asks Velma.

"We saw a little boy in a window of the East Wing," says Shaggy. "You know, the closed-off part of the mansion. He was dressed like he was from a couple hundred years ago."

"Sounds like a mystery to me," says Fred.

"Like, why does he always have to say stuff like that?" Shaggy asks Scooby.

Scooby just shrugs as the duo follow the rest of their gang back inside the mansion.

Turn the page.

Inside the building, the gang casually strolls over to the roped-off East Wing, so as not to raise suspicion. Fred waits until the elderly man behind the information desk isn't looking.

"Come on!" he whispers to his friends.

The gang hops the rope and darts into the closed portion of the mansion.

The first room in the East Wing is a large ballroom. Furniture is covered with white tarps. Bright squares of paint reveal where paintings used to hang, protecting the small sections of wall from the Sun's rays piercing in through the skylight. An eerie sense of quiet fills the hall. That is, until Velma sees a small figure walk past a doorway at the ballroom's opposite end.

"There!" she shouts.

Turn to page 82.

"Look at the floor, Fred," says Daphne.

"What is that?" Fred says. He walks to the center of the elaborately painted room. He crouches down to get a better look. There are train tracks that cross the entire floor. Surprisingly, the tracks are solid metal, mounted on aged wood. There is even a thin layer of rust built up on them, as if they have been used outside for decades.

"Isn't that strange?" Daphne asks. "And look where they lead."

Fred does just that and notices that the tracks head into a dark tunnel at the far side of the room. The tunnel looks like it's made of solid stone. He looks at Daphne and she shrugs. The two follow the tracks under the stone archway and into the shadows.

Turn to page 77

The end of the tunnel is completely dark, but Fred and Daphne keep shuffling forward anyway.

"There!" says Daphne. "Up ahead."

At first, Fred thinks the light appearing down the tunnel is the exit. But as it gets bigger and bigger, he suddenly realizes it's a different kind of light altogether. Although it seems impossible, a train is heading right for them.

Fred turns to run, but Daphne pulls at his sleeve. "Here!" she shouts over the roar of the oncoming locomotive. Just as the train is about to hit them, she pushes Fred to the side. The two collide with a hidden door and knock it open.

Daphne slams the door closed behind them. "What is going on?" she yells.

"I think we may have our answer," Fred says.

All around Fred and Daphne are high-tech cameras and projection equipment.

"Well, what did you think?" says a woman's voice behind them. "Welcome to my house of horrors."

Turn the page.

Fred and Daphne turn to see an older woman walk toward them. "My special effects have made this place a certified tourist attraction. The Mayhem Mansion, they call it. I couldn't have thought of a better title myself."

"Tina Mayhew," says Daphne.

"That's right," says Ms. Mayhew with a big grin on her face. "And I guess now my secret's out."

"You seem surprisingly happy about that," says Fred.

"It was only a matter of time, really," Tina Mayhew says. "Just be sure when you tell the press, you mention how good my effects look."

As Tina leads Fred and Daphne toward the exit, the two exchange a glance. They aren't sure if they've just experienced genius or a train wreck.

THE END

To follow another path, turn to page 12.

To Velma's surprise, the glowing light is gone. The woman looks completely normal.

"What happened?" says the guide. She shakes her head, as if to clear it.

"You don't remember?" asks Velma. "You were possessed, or at least that's what it looked like."

"I was?" says the tour guide. "And people still don't believe this place is haunted. But you believe, don't you?"

But Velma doesn't answer. She just gives the guide a polite smile.

Velma follows the other tourists as they shuffle downstairs toward the gift shop or the parking lot. Then she doubles back to the stairway. She sprints upstairs. There, mounted on the wall, she sees what she's looking for. She opens a glass case and removes a fire extinguisher.

In a hurry, Velma heads back up to the rooftop patio and hides behind a large potted plant.

Turn the page.

". . . the Mayhews' attempts at making the mansion a virtual maze of clashing designs and winding hallways, hundreds of these ghost stories still abound," says the familiar monotone of the tour guide as she steps out onto the rooftop a few minutes later.

The guide walks across the patio and says, "In fact, some guests report there being possess—." It seems history is repeating itself. The guide's eyes begin to glow bright white.

"Possess*IONS!*" she says as her voice changes to that odd, deep tone.

"Ha!" Velma yells as she jumps out from behind the plant.

She aims the fire extinguisher at the guide and squeezes the trigger. *ZZZAAAZZZZ!*

Sparks fly from the tour guide's shirt. Velma releases the trigger on the extinguisher and the spray stops. *CLANK!*

A small electronic device falls to the floor. The tour guide's eyes are no longer glowing white.

"I knew it from the moment she fell down," says Velma to the rest of the Mystery Inc. gang as they all climb in their famous van a short time later. "She made a *clank* noise when she hit the ground. Like something metal was in her shirt. Turns out it was some sort of lighting device that made her appear to glow."

"So she was just scaring tourists to get more visitors to the mansion?" asks Daphne.

"Exactly," says Velma. "And it was working. The whole management team was in on it."

"I wonder how news of this will affect business?" says Fred.

"Well, there's no such thing as bad press," says Daphne.

"Yeah, just bad electronics," says Velma as the Mystery Machine drives away.

THE END

To follow another path, turn to page 12.

The gang runs across the ballroom and through a small stairwell. Down at the opposite end of a long hallway is a large wooden door. The floor is tiled with black and white panels. They seem to bring even more attention to the lone doorway.

"Let's go!" says Fred. The gang sprints across the hall, Scooby and Shaggy taking up the rear.

As they continue down the long corridor, Scooby notices the ceiling getting lower. The walls also seem to be getting closer and closer together. It isn't long before the rest of the gang realizes this, too.

"The hallway's getting smaller!" Daphne says.

"It's some kind of optical illusion," adds Velma.

"Roptical rirusion?" asks Scooby, as the gang stops.

"From the other end, the hallway looks normal," says Velma. "But when we walk through it, we see that it's actually getting smaller. It's called forced perspective."

"Forced perspective or not, we can't afford to slow down now," says Fred. He drops to his knees and begins to crawl toward the door. The ceiling is so low now that he doesn't have any other choice.

The rest of the gang follows as Fred pushes open the door, which in reality is not much larger than a doggie door.

"Hey!" Fred yells.

The Mystery Inc. gang has discovered the little "ghost" boy as he stands in an otherwise empty room. The boy looks a little sad and is wearing old-fashioned clothes that look to be from around the late 1800s.

"I'm lost," says the little boy from across the empty room.

"Zoinks!" says Shaggy. "Isn't this house designed so wonky to confuse lost spirits? Now it's trapped one!"

"Calm down, Shaggy," says Velma. She turns to the little boy. "What's your name?"

Turn to page 85.

"Brian," says the boy. I was here with my parents. We came right after play rehearsal at school. And now I'm lost."

"Which is why you're dressed in old-fashioned clothes," says Daphne.

The gang happily leads the little boy back to the lobby, where they find his anxious parents at the front desk. As the parents hug their little boy, the gang leaves the mansion.

"We may not have solved all the mysteries of this place," says Fred, "but we did something a little more important."

"Like, yeah," says Shaggy. "We got all the ghost hunting out of the way, so now we can finally have dinner!"

THE END

To follow another path, turn to page 12.

As Fred and Daphne begin to descend the staircase, Fred glances back over his shoulder. There, on one of the bizarre sideways staircases, walks a glowing white figure. He appears to be dressed in an old-fashioned set of tights, like a Shakespearian actor. His face is long and hollow. His eyes stare back at Fred with an inhuman glow about them.

"How is he doing that?" asks Fred under his breath.

Daphne looks over to see what Fred is talking about.

"That can't be real!" says Daphne.

Neither moves, as they watch the figure do the seemingly impossible. Then, without warning, the ghostly man screams.

AAAGGGHHH!

Daphne is the first one down the stairs. Fred follows soon afterward. When he checks back over his shoulder, he sees the pale ghost following him, walking on the ceiling now. The ghost is stepping quickly but carefully. All the while, his eyes stare at the young couple with a sad, blank expression. It is almost hypnotic to Fred. He finds it hard to look away.

"This house is insane!" Daphne says as the two run down the hallway away from the apparition. On either side of them are portholes, like those found in the side of an old-fashioned submarine. The portholes each house a small aquarium. Combined with the nautical decor, the entire hallway seems as if it is underwater.

Daphne and Fred do their best to ignore the setting. They open a hatch at the end of the hall and step through it.

Turn the page.

With no sign of the ghost, Daphne and Fred take a quick second to catch their breath. Fred looks around. The two have wandered into one of the mansion's greenhouses.

"I remember seeing this room listed on the tour," says Daphne.

"Now that you mention it . . . , " says Fred as he points toward a doorway across the room. Shuffling past the door is a tour group not unlike the one they had parted ways with earlier.

"Well, at least we don't have to worry about that ghost now," says Daphne as she and Fred head toward the group. "I doubt he'd show himself with so many witnesses around."

All of a sudden, once again, the sound of screaming echoes down the hallway.

SCREEEAM!

Turn to page 96.

To Velma, it seems like the other tourists have the right idea. She turns and runs away from the glowing white tour guide. As quickly as she can, she sprints down the staircase. Behind her, she can hear another set of hurried footsteps. Giving in to curiosity, Velma looks back. She instantly regrets her decision. Rushing toward her is the guide. White light pours from her eyes and mouth.

"How dare you trespass on my family's sacred ground!" the guide's now-deep voice screams. "Leave my home at once!"

Right at that moment, there is nothing Velma wants to do more than take the ghost's suggestion.

Turn the page.

There's only one problem. The Mayhem Mansion got its nickname from its weird architecture. Very few people can navigate its halls without getting lost. In fact, Velma had read about a family that had wandered through its maze-like rooms for over a day before finding its way to the exit. And while Velma had paid attention during the tour, after running through a few unmarked rooms to flee the possessed guide, she's now totally and completely lost.

Unfortunately, the ghost doesn't have the same issue.

Velma runs through a set of connecting bedrooms, but the tour guide is fast on her heels. She's only a room or so behind Velma, and doesn't look to be slowing down anytime soon.

"Get out!" shouts the guide.

"I'm trying!" Velma says.

Velma slams open the door in front of her. She looks around, wondering which way to go next. She's found her way to the kitchen, but that doesn't do her any good. She runs over the slick tile and into the next room. It's a long, skinny pantry. At its opposite end are two doors.

Velma throws both open. One is simply a walk-in closet containing a host of cleaning supplies. A mop is dislodged from its place resting against the wall. It falls to the ground in front of Velma. She only sees it from the corner of her eye and jumps back. Her heart is nearly beating out of her chest. She steadies herself and then looks over toward the other door. It leads downstairs to a lower level.

Purposely leaving the stairwell door open, Velma slides into the closet. She shuts the door behind her and waits in the dark room.

Turn to page 99.

"That's it!" says Shaggy. "That's enough spooky encounters for one afternoon!"

He and Scooby jump out of their chairs at the café. They run toward the exit, almost knocking over their waitress who is carrying their order of a dozen hot dogs on her tray. But right as they approach the front hedge, they see the slender "ghost" waiter walking toward them.

"The other way!" Shaggy says. "Go back, Scoobs!"

He and Scooby turn so abruptly, they're surprised when they both manage to stay on their feet. They run back toward the café, and past the waitress still carrying their hot dogs. But this time, they just miss her and she drops the tray. Scooby barely has time to gobble up a few of the fallen frankfurters before he catches back up to Shaggy and they round the side of the mansion.

Turn the page.

Scooby-Doo and Shaggy keep running past a hedge maze and a gardener's shack before they both need to stop for a little air. As they pant, they look around the garden. Dozens of hedges carved to look like animals stand on every side. There are elephants, dolphins, and even a hedge that looks like a palm tree hosting a swinging monkey.

"Pretty cool, huh, Scoobs?" says Shaggy after he catches his breath.

"Reah!" says Scooby. Then a figure pops his head out from behind a giant hedge swan. "Ro!" Scooby yells in fear.

"You shouldn't be here!" says the man in a gravelly voice. He's short and stubby, but his face carries the same emotionless expression as the boy they had glimpsed in the window.

"Yikes!" Shaggy exclaims.

Running out of directions to run, Scooby and Shaggy see a side door to the mansion just a few yards away.

"Like, that-a-way, Scoobs!" Shaggy yells.

They sprint to the door and fling it open. Then they leap inside. They skid along a polished marble floor until they come to a stop by two equally polished leather shoes.

"Can I help you?" says a familiar voice.

Scooby and Shaggy look up and see the elderly man who usually sits at the mansion's information desk.

"Rary Rardener!" says Scooby.

"Excuse me?" says the man.

"Like, we saw a scary gardener outside," says Shaggy. "Please tell me he works here and is not another creepy ghost!"

Turn to page 103.

"So much for that theory," says Fred. He and Daphne step out into the hall to join the tour. The strange, white ghost blocks the group's path. His arms are outstretched as he hangs from the ceiling. The tourists are scattering in any direction they can. The entire scene is one of pure chaos.

"Looks like our ghost isn't afraid of crowds after all," says Daphne.

Hearing Daphne's words, the ghost cranes his neck toward her. Then his body begins to float down the hall in her direction, all the while remaining upside down.

"Uh-oh!" Fred says, as he and Daphne begin to back up.

"Wait!" says Fred. He reaches out and grabs Daphne's arm to hold her in place. He nods upward, and Daphne looks at the ceiling.

"Huh," Daphne says. She also stands her ground.

The ghost floats closer down the hall, but neither of the teens moves a muscle. Then the ghost stops. It just hangs there, a few feet away from them. Then it starts to struggle, pulling at its own feet.

Daphne smiles and casually walks up to the ghost. Its eyes continue to glow, but she doesn't seem to mind.

She slowly reaches her hand up to its face.

"Some ghost," says Daphne as she pulls off the strange figure's glowing mask.

Hanging there from the ceiling is an older man, still very much alive. Up close, the rope the man used to glide down the hallway is even more obvious. Fred had noticed that there was a knot in the rope. Knowing the "ghost's" rig would get stuck on it, all he and Daphne had to do was wait.

Turn the page.

"Timothy Mayhew?" asks Daphne.

"Yes, you've caught me," says the man. "I faked my own death years ago to live in peace away from the public eye. But when they turned my home into a tourist attraction, I had no choice but to resort to my old circus roots to scare away the visitors."

As Daphne and Fred go to let the rest of the Mystery Inc. gang know the mystery has been solved, they hear the hum of cameras. The rest of the tourists have discovered Timothy Mayhew.

The bright lights of dozens of flashes sparkle in the hallway behind Fred and Daphne. Like it or not, Mayhew is once again the star of the show.

THE END

To follow another path, turn to page 12.

There's the sound of footsteps from the other side of the closet door. Velma holds her breath and waits.

"You can't hide from me!" shouts the deep voice of the tour guide. "I have walked these halls for generations!"

Velma doesn't say anything. She leans against the door of the closet, listening closely. Her eyes widen as she sees the doorknob to the closet begin to turn.

"Are you in—" the guide starts to say. "Ha!"

The doorknob stops turning.

There's a long pause. Velma closes her eyes.

"You would do better to cover your tracks!" the guide says.

Turn the page.

Velma hears the tour guide's footsteps as she descends the nearby stairs. Leaving the door open worked! The possessed guide thinks she's downstairs. Velma lets out a sigh. She's lost the tour guide, but how is she ever going to get herself out of this place?

CLUNK! CLUNK! CLUNK!

There are footsteps again on the steps. Velma's heart starts pounding nearly out of her chest. Has the guide come back?

"Jinkies!" Velma says to herself in a hushed whisper.

She looks around inside the closet. There's no escape. She's trapped herself. She grabs a broom, if only to be armed with something.

The doorknob slowly turns. The door opens.

Turn to page 102.

"You're not supposed to be in here," says a large security guard.

It takes a second for Velma to open her eyes at the sound of the unfamiliar voice.

"Excuse me?" she says.

"No tourists in the kitchen area," says the security guard. "What is it with you kids today?"

Velma doesn't say anything, but she gets to her feet.

"I already banned that redheaded girl and her blond friend. Not to mention that weird talking dog with the skinny kid," says the guard. "Let me guess, you're with them?"

Velma smiles weakly, but she still doesn't say anything. Instead, she lets the guard escort her outside the mansion's grounds. She doesn't feel like talking. She just wants to be safely inside the Mystery Machine and as far away from the Mayhem Mansion as humanly possible.

THE END

To follow another path, turn to page 12.

"Why, my dear boy," says the elderly man, "there are no gardeners here today. They only come in on the weekends."

"What?!" Shaggy says, getting to his feet.

"There are no maids here either," says the old man. "But there used to be a full staff working every day of the week back in the 1800s."

"*Yikes!*" says Shaggy.

"The closest exit is through those doors," says the old man. "Thanks for visiting the Mayhew Mansion."

Scooby and Shaggy look at each other. Then they hurry through the door across the room.

"Let's get out of here, Scoobs!" says Shaggy as the two run down a hall.

Turn the page.

There's a glowing exit sign at the other end. Both Shaggy and Scooby are relieved to see it.

Suddenly a figure steps out of one of the many doorways lining the hallway. She's dressed in a maid's uniform. Scooby and Shaggy stop in their tracks.

"Oh, man!" says Shaggy. "That old guy said there was no cleaning staff working today!"

The woman looks at Shaggy and Scooby with a blank expression on her face. No one moves. Then suddenly a few other maids pop their heads out of nearby doorways.

"Zoinks!" says Shaggy. "It's like a ghost army!"

He and Scooby do a quick about-face and head back the way they came.

It takes a few twists and turns, but finally, Scooby and Shaggy find their way into the mansion's lobby once again.

"Stop right there!" shouts the elderly man, now once again behind the information desk.

"Gotcha!" the old man says. Then he smiles.

"Got what now?" asks Shaggy.

"I hope you'll forgive me, but I'm a prankster at heart," says the old man. "It runs in my blood. After all, I am a Mayhew. I come from a long line of comedians."

Scooby and Shaggy look at each other. They're not sure what to think.

"The waiter, the gardener, the maids," says the old man. "Of course we have a full staff. Have you seen how big this place is?"

"So it was all a joke?" says Shaggy. "Even the creepy little ghost boy we saw in the window?"

"What ghost boy?" asks the old man.

He might have been smiling, but Shaggy and Scooby don't wait to see if the elderly man is still joking with them. They are halfway to the Mystery Machine before they even turn around. They've had quite enough of the Mayhem Mansion for one day.

THE END

To follow another path, turn to page 12.

AUTHOR

Matthew K. Manning is the author of the best-selling books *Batman: A Visual History*, *The Batman Files*, and *The Superman Files*. Matthew was one of the regular writers for the DC comic book series Beware the Batman, The Batman Strikes!, and Legion of Super-Heroes in the 31st Century. Currently writing for IDW's Teenage Mutant Ninja Turtles: Amazing Adventures, Matthew has also written comics or books starring Spider-Man, Wonder Woman, Wolverine, Iron Man, Captain America, the Flash, Thor, Green Lantern, the Justice League, the X-Men, Hulk, Scooby-Doo, and Looney Tunes. He currently resides in Asheville, North Carolina, with his wife, Dorothy, and their two daughters, Lillian and Gwendolyn.

ILLUSTRATOR

Scott Neely has been a professional illustrator and designer for many years. Since 1999, he's been an official Scooby-Doo and Cartoon Network artist, working on such licensed properties as Dexter's Laboratory, Johnny Bravo, Courage the Cowardly Dog, Powerpuff Girls, and more. He has also worked on Pokémon, Mickey Mouse Clubhouse, My Friends Tigger & Pooh, Handy Manny, Strawberry Shortcake, Bratz, and many other popular characters. He lives in a suburb of Philadelphia.

GLOSSARY

apparition (ap-uh-RISH-uhn)—sudden vision, especially of a ghost

art deco (ART DEK-oh)—style of art or architecture that was popular in the 1930s

eccentric (ek-SEN-trik)—peculiar or unusual, different from usual

intricately (IN-truh-kit-lee)—having lots of parts or elements in something

monotone (MON-uh-tohn)—sound that does not change in tone or pitch

nautical (NAW-tuh-kuhl)—relating to sailors, ships, or navigation

ominous (OM-uh-nuhss)—threatening evil

séance (SAY-ahns)—meeting to communicate with spirits

silhouette (sill-oo-ET)—portrait in profile, showing a face from the side

stalactite (stuh-LAK-tite)—long chunk of calcium carbonate rock that hangs from the roof of caves

stalagmite (stuh-LAG-mite)—long chunk of calcium carbonate rock that points up from the floor of caves

superstitious (soo-per-STISH-us)—having a fear of the mysterious or unknown

YOU CHOOSE JOKES!

YOU CHOOSE which punch line is funniest!

Why didn't Fred and Shaggy go inside the haunted house?

a. It was **Wednesday** and the house is only open on **Frightday!**

b. They had ghost-aphobia!

c. I don't know. Everyone else is dying to go in!

What did the angry candle say to the other candle?

a. "You're fired!"

b. "Don't get short with me!"

c. "You think you're so bright, don't you?"

When is the best time to see a ghost?

a. In the moaning!

b. The dead of night!

c. After dinner, when it's clear they've eaten!

How can you tell if the house next door is haunted?

a. It only opens with a skeleton key!

b. You can hear coffin inside!

c. It doesn't have a living room!

Did you hear about the party at the haunted mansion?

a. No one could decide who was the ghost of honor!

b. It was so noisy, the neighbors called the police in-specter!

c. The witches got too rowdy so they were ex-spelled!

How do you keep cool in a haunted house?

a. With scare-conditioner!

b. Plug in an electric fan-tom!

c. Have some I-scream!

LOOK FOR MORE...

← YOU CHOOSE →

SCOOBY-DOO!

THE CHOICE IS YOURS!